S0-AND-677

SHORT TALES CLASSICS

Johann David Wyss's

Shipwrecked

Adapted by John Helfers
Illustrated by John Cboins

GREEN LEVEL

- Familiar topics
- Frequently used words
- Repeating language patterns

BLUE LEVEL

- New ideas introduced
- Larger vocabulary
- Variety of language patterns

PINK LEVEL

- More complex ideas
- Extended vocabulary
- Expanded sentence structures

To learn more about Short Tales leveling, go to www.abdopublishing.com

---

Published by Magic Wagon, a division of the ABDO Publishing Group, 8000 West 78th Street, Edina, Minnesota, 55439.

Printed in the United States.

Written by Johann David Wyss
Adapted Text by John Helfers
Illustrations by John Cboins
Colors by Wes Hartman
Edited by Stephanie Hedlund
Interior Layout by Kristen Fitzner Denton
Book Design and Packaging by Shannon Eric Denton

Library of Congress Cataloging-in-Publication Data
Helfers, John.
Johann David Wyss' the Swiss family Robinson : shipwrecked! / adapted by John Helfers ; illustrated by John Cboins.
p. cm. -- (Short tales classics)
ISBN 978-1-60270-122-9
[1. Shipwrecks--Fiction. 2. Survival--Fiction.] I. Cboins, John, ill.
II. Wyss, Johann David, 1743-1818. Schweizerische Robinson. English. III.
Title. IV. Title: Swiss family Robinson. V. Title: Shipwreck!
PZ7.H37385Jo 2008
[Fic]--dc22

2007036970

Contents

CHAPTER ONE: THE STORM

My name is Johann Robinson.

In 1799, I set out with my family from England to Australia to make a new life.

But our ship ran into a terrible storm while at sea.

We were tossed about for six days and nights!

For our safety, we stayed in our cabin.
And, it soon seemed that we had been forgotten.

I heard a cry of "Land! Land!" Just then the boat shook and came to a stop.

I went on deck to see what was happening. The ship was caught on the large rock.

Off in the distance, I saw land.

But, I found no one on deck.

The captain and crew had abandoned us!

Returning to my family, I said, "Take courage! Tomorrow we will attempt to reach land."

During the night, wave after wave crashed against the ship. We could hear planks tear away from the hull.

At last, our five children were all asleep. My wife and I spent the long night waiting for dawn.

CHAPTER TWO: SCAVENGING

The next morning, we all went outside.

My children crowded around, asking what we were going to do.

I replied, "Let us all consider what is best to do now."

“We can swim to shore,” cried 15-year-old Fritz.

“Very well for you,” replied 12-year-old Ernest. “You can swim. Would it not be better to construct a raft and go all together?”

“That might do,” I said. “Away, and seek for anything that may be useful.”

We all went to different parts of the ship.

I went to find food and water.

My wife went to care for the livestock.

Fritz looked for arms and ammunition.

Ernest searched for tools.

Ten-year-old Jack went to the captain's cabin.

Upon opening the door, he was knocked over by two large dogs.

Jack rode the largest up to me, to show me what he found.

My family had found many tools and two rifles.

Francis, our youngest, brought a box of pointed hooks.

When his brothers laughed, I frowned at them.

"These fishhooks may be more useful than anything else on the ship," I said.

My wife joined us as well.

“I have found a cow, a donkey, two goats, six sheep, and a sow with her young. I have fed them, and I hope that we may bring them.”

"Very well," I said. " I am pleased with all but Master Jack! He has contributed nothing but two great eaters."

"They can help us to hunt when we get to land," said Jack.

"Yes," I replied. "But how are we to get there?"

CHAPTER THREE: BUILDING THE RAFT

"We can float to shore," he replied.

I smiled. "A very good idea, Jack. Give me the saw!"

We found several large wooden casks. They were perfect for our needs.

We brought them up and began to saw them all in half.

I found a long, flexible plank. Then I nailed the eight tubs in a row.

Next, we nailed a plank to each side.

When we were done, we had formed a boat with eight compartments.

Our new vessel was so heavy that we could not budge it.

So, I lifted the front with some rope.

Then, I placed some rollers under it.

With the help of the boys, we launched the raft.

I wanted to steady the boat even more.

So, I attached a pole to the front and one to the back.

This kept the raft steady.

By the time we had finished, the sun was setting. We were forced to spend another night on the wrecked ship.

We ate dinner and went to bed.

"Give the animals food for some days. If we are successful, we may return for them," I said early the next morning.

"Collect what you wish to carry away. But choose only things absolutely necessary for survival."

Our first load included the guns and ammunition.
We also took some food, an iron pot, and a fishing rod.

A chest of nails and carpenter tools joined the other items.
Then we added a sailcloth to make a tent.

We were finally ready to leave when the roosters crowed!

We placed ten hens and two roosters in a covered pen.

We set the rest free, hoping they might get themselves to shore.

CHAPTER FOUR: SETTING SAIL

At last, we were ready to leave.

We carefully climbed in our raft and set out.

Each of us held an oar and rowed with all our might.

At first, the boat kept turning. And we made no progress.

Finally I got the hang of steering.

When they saw us go, the dogs leaped into the sea.

I feared they would tip the boat. So, I couldn't let them come aboard.

But by resting their paws on the outriggers, they kept up with us.

All around us were barrels, bales, and chests from the wreck.
Fritz and I managed to grab two casks. We tied them to our raft and towed them behind us.

Soon, Fritz's sharp eyes spotted coconut trees on the shore. I wished I had brought the captain's telescope.

Just then, Jack produced a smaller one from his pocket.

With it, I spotted a small bay of smooth water. We rowed toward it.

As soon as the raft hit the beach, we all waded ashore.

The boys began chattering and the animals joined in. It was a welcome ruckus.

It meant we had all made it safely to this desert island! We were together and alive!